Eaglet's World

WRITTEN BY **Evelyn Minshull**   ILLUSTRATED BY **Andrea Gabriel**

ALBERT WHITMAN & COMPANY, MORTON GROVE, ILLINOIS

For Jonathan and Benjamin Hittie. — E. M.

To Connie, Ashley, and Roshni — for being my friends
during good times and bad. — A. G.

Library of Congress Cataloging-in-Publication Data
Minshull, Evelyn White.
Eaglet's world / by Evelyn Minshull ; illustrated by Andrea Gabriel.
p. cm.
Summary: From the time he is still in the egg, a baby bald eagle is
reluctant to take each new step in his growth, until the day comes when
he flies and sees the beautiful world beyond his parents' nest.
ISBN 0-8075-8929-2 (hardcover)
ISBN 0-8075-1760-7 (paperback)
1. Bald eagle — Juvenile fiction.   [1. Bald eagle — Fiction.
2. Eagles — Fiction.   3. Growth — Fiction.   4. Flight — Fiction.
5. Animals — Habits and behavior — Fiction.]   I. Gabriel, Andrea, ill.
II. Title.   PZ10.3.M632 Eag 2002   [E] — dc21   2001004093

The design is by Scott Piehl.

For more information visit our web site at www.albertwhitman.com

Where Eaglet was . . . was cozy.
It was dark and damp and warm.

When Eaglet moved, he touched slippery smoothness.
Sometimes, he felt movement above . . . a jostling . . .
a gentle rocking.
He heard whirring . . . quiet murmurs.
What could it be? *Where* could it be?
Would he ever go there?
He cuddled in dark, warm softness.
He didn't want to go anywhere.
Not now. Not ever.
Where he was . . . was cozy.

But one day, where Eaglet was . . . was too small.

His wings pressed against hard roundness. His beak clicked.
Click-click. Click-click-click.

Faster and faster he pecked.

He decided to discover what lay beyond that familiar smoothness!

For where Eaglet was . . . was too small.

Where Eaglet was . . . was safe.
The nest was deep and sturdy.
Rough twigs made it strong; down made it soft and cuddly.
His mother's and father's wings kept him warm.

Sometimes, their wings whirred;
they lifted off the nest, taking warmth with them.
Then, Eaglet learned, there would soon be food.

He opened his beak wide for wriggling insects,
or soft, mushy grubs, or small, firm fragments of fish.
He would stay here forever. Forever.
Where he was . . . was warm and safe.

Where Eaglet was . . . was becoming crowded.

Once, the nest had seemed huge.

Now, he felt scrunched between his parents.

Sometimes sharp twigs jabbed him.

When his mother and father left him alone, he wondered. . .

What was it like beyond the rough rim of the nest?

Stretching his neck, he saw blue-blue-blue everywhere,

and his parents flying closer. Food! Food for him!

He didn't need blueness.

He'd stay in this nest forever,

forever,

even though where he was . . . was becoming crowded.

Where Eaglet was . . . was frightening!
His parents had coaxed him to the edge of the nest.
He didn't like it there. He clutched twigs with his talons
as the wind rocked him back and forth, back and forth.
It was cool and stroking. It ruffled his feathers.
What was it? he wondered.
He didn't want to know.
He wanted the deep, safe, crowded nest.

But his mother kept prodding him gently.
Spreading his wings, his father moved outward into blueness,
then back again. Surely they didn't expect him to follow!

He didn't want to! He wouldn't!
He wouldn't leave the nest.
Never. Never.

They showed him again. How easy it looked—for *them!*
Couldn't they see that his wings weren't as wide as theirs?
He felt himself wobbling.
He'd fall! He just knew it!
He didn't want to fly. He wanted things to be as they had been.
Forever. Forever.

His mother nudged him, and suddenly he could no longer feel the nest.
He screamed, for where he was . . .

was terribly frightening.

He scrambled in nothingness,
but his mother and father were there.
Their wings would keep him from falling.
He felt cool air beneath his own wings, catching them. Lifting them.
And, surprisingly . . .

where Eaglet was . . . was wonderful!

He saw a wider, deeper blue than he might ever have imagined
from within his safe, warm nest.
He felt such brightness as he could never have guessed
in the dark, damp coziness of the egg.
Below him stretched mountains, glistening with white,
shadowed blue and purple . . .

and between the mountains spread greenness . . .
and a river glinting as it wound among rocks
and through deep valleys.
Clouds drifted. Breezes whispered.
Wind whistled as it carried Eaglet, his wingtips tilted in soaring.
The world was huge! And it was all his!

He would soar there above it, surprised by its bigness,
its color and brightness,
forever! Forever!
Where Eaglet was . . .

was *wonderful!*

About Bald Eagles

Beautiful, graceful, and powerful, bald eagles average flying speeds of thirty miles an hour, though their wings can appear nearly motionless in flight. The outspread wings of an adult eagle often measure seven feet from wingtip to wingtip.

Bald eagles can be found all over North America. Many migrate to warmer climates in the fall, sometimes "visiting" an area for weeks before moving on to their warmer winter destination. In the spring, however, they are quick to return north to their nesting areas.

An eagles' nest — also called an *aerie* — is usually around five feet in diameter, but may grow to as much as nine feet as the birds add on to it over the years. Eagles prefer high, quiet places such as treetops or cliffs, and they like to build their nests near rivers or coasts. Eagle parents breed once a year — sometimes only once every few years — and mothers typically lay one or two eggs.

When eaglets are first hatched, they are soft and grayish-white, weak and helpless — but by the time they are about a month old, they are able to stand and shred food. As the young eagles grow, mottled dark and white feathers replace their fuzzy down.

When their flying feathers are fully formed, between ten and thirteen weeks after hatching, eaglets attempt flight. Though the eaglets mature quickly and soon learn to fly and hunt like their parents, their head and tail feathers do not turn white until their fourth year. If they survive the dangers of the wild, bald eagles can live up to thirty years or more.

Greater dangers have come from people. The poisons found in pesticides such as DDT have proven harmful to eagles, and in the past many eagles were victims of trappers and bounty hunters. As a result, the bald eagle population decreased to the point that they were — and still are — considered an endangered species. Government regulations were created to protect them, and eagle populations are now increasing at a rapid rate nationwide. Sightings of bald eagles are becoming more common, especially near bodies of water.

Throughout history, from ancient Rome to Native American cultures to modern times, humans have been in awe of the speed and sheer grace of these majestic birds. While there are nearly sixty species of eagles worldwide, the bald eagle is most familiar to North America — especially to the United States, where, as national bird, it continues to inspire thoughts of strength and freedom.